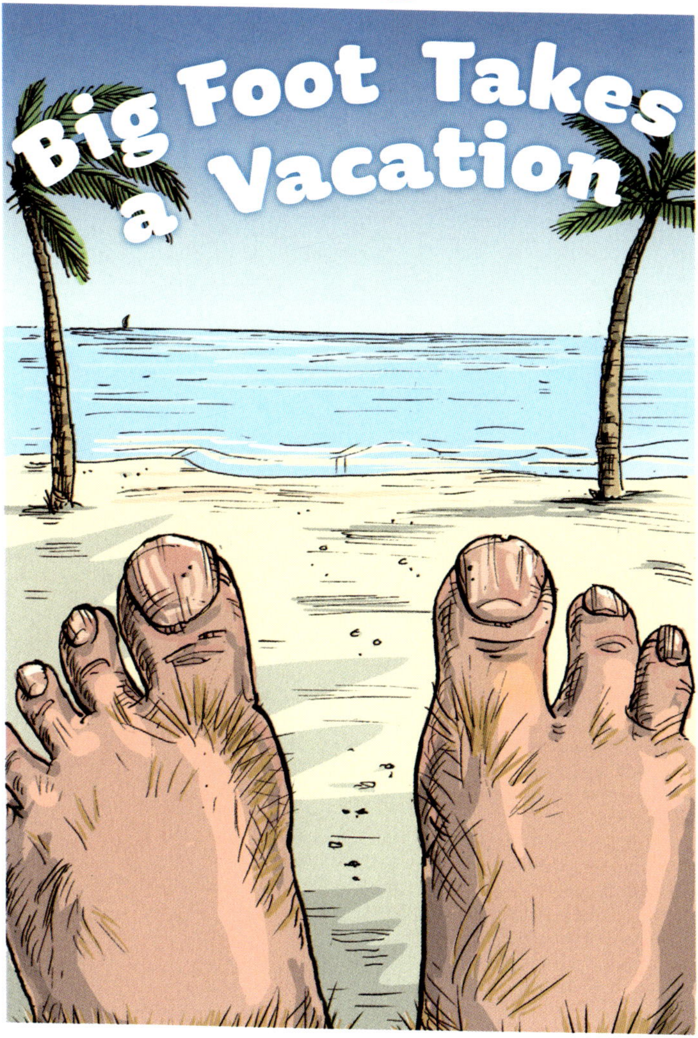
Big Foot Takes
a Vacation

By Dona Herweck Rice
Illustrated by Sholto Walker

Consultant
Kristin Risdahl, M.S.Ed.
K–12 Social Studies Instructional Facilitator
Knox County Schools, Tennessee

Publishing Credits
Rachelle Cracchiolo, M.S.Ed., *Publisher*
Emily R. Smith, M.A.Ed., *VP of Content Development*
Véronique Bos, *Creative Director*
Dani Neiley, *Associate Editor*
Kevin Pham, *Graphic Designer*

Image Credits
Illustrated by Sholto Walker

Library of Congress Cataloging-in-Publication Data
Names: Rice, Dona, author. | Walker, Sholto, illustrator.
Title: Big Foot takes a vacation / by Dona Herweck Rice ; illustrated by Sholto Walker.
Description: Huntington Beach, CA : Teacher Created Materials, [2022] | Audience: Grades 2-3. | Summary: "Frank is tired of being called Big Foot! And he's tired of everyone trying to sneak a photo of him. He needs a break. A vacation is just the thing. Frank packs his bag and goes on an adventure. Watch out everyone...Big Foot is coming!"-- Provided by publisher.
Identifiers: LCCN 2022005978 (print) | LCCN 2022005979 (ebook) | ISBN 9781087605401 (paperback) | ISBN 9781087632261 (ebook)
Subjects: LCSH: Readers (Primary) | LCGFT: Readers (Publications)
Classification: LCC PE1119.2 .R532 2022 (print) | LCC PE1119.2 (ebook) | DDC 428.6/2--dc23/eng/20220217
LC record available at https://lccn.loc.gov/2022005978
LC ebook record available at https://lccn.loc.gov/2022005979

5482 Argosy Avenue
Huntington Beach, CA 92649
www.tcmpub.com

ISBN 978-1-0876-0540-1
© 2023 Teacher Created Materials, Inc.

This book may not be reproduced or distributed in any way without prior written consent from the publisher.

Printed by 51250
PO 10851 / Printed in USA

Table of Contents

Chapter One:
   Frank..............................4

Chapter Two:
   See the World 12

Chapter Three:
   Get the Picture 18

Chapter Four:
   Frank Lands on His Feet 26

About Us 32

Chapter One

Frank

Frank *knew* he had big feet. He had big hands, a big head, big legs, and big arms. His fingers were big, his nose was big, and his big ears stuck out left and right. And yes, his tummy was big, too. It was easy to see that Frank was a very big guy.

So, why, oh why, did they have to call him Big *Foot*? First, it was Big Frank, but then that wasn't good enough. Big Foot. Oh, they laughed when they came up with that one. Big Foot? I mean, can you imagine? Big Foot!

Oh, the indignity of it all.

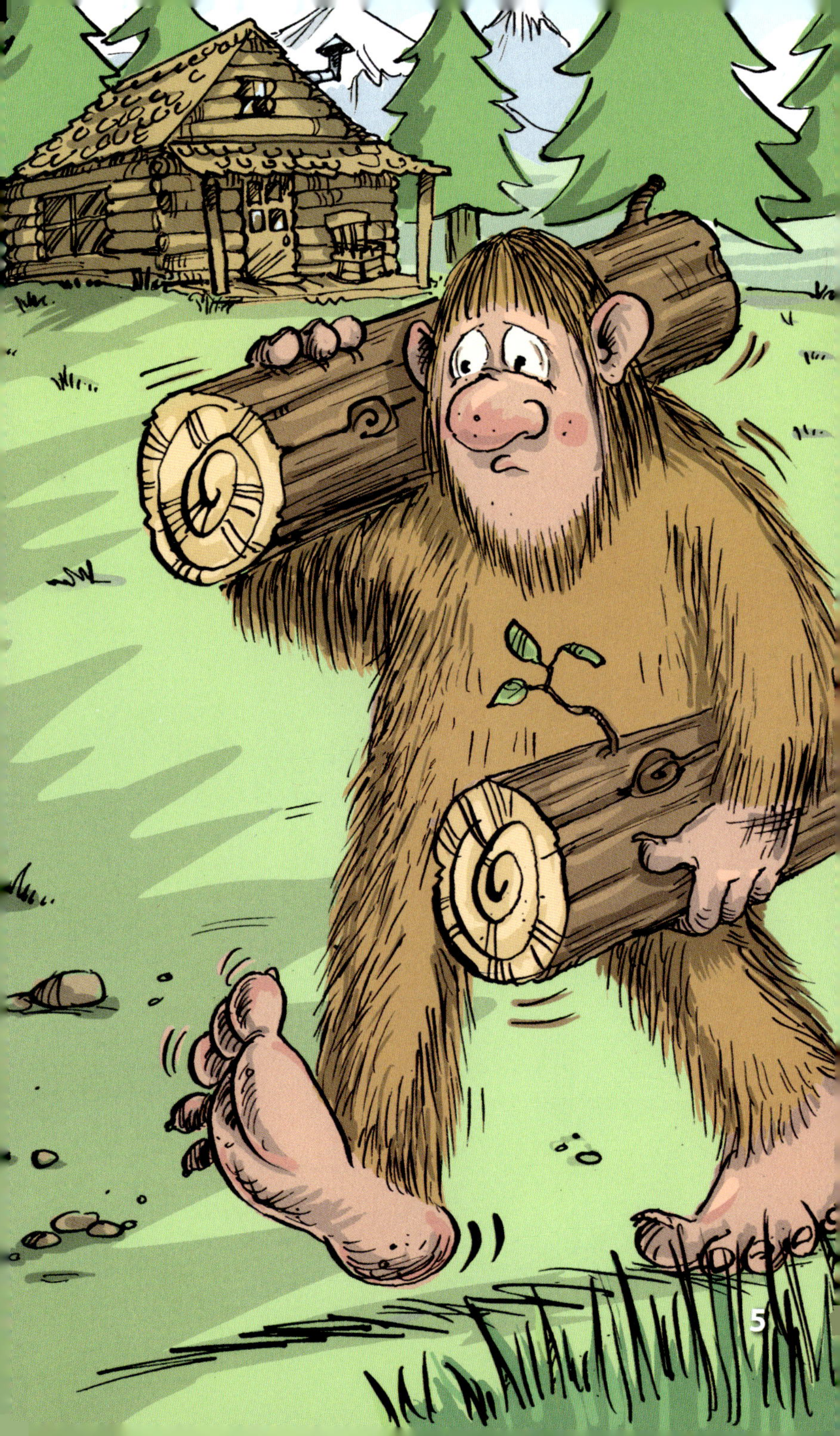

They were so focused on his "bigness" that they never noticed his conversation skills. His fancy footwork on the dance floor went totally unnoticed as well. And the perfectly flaky crust on his homemade cherry pie never even got a mention.

Oh, no, they just wanted him to stomp around the wilderness and keep the tourists coming. Everyone wanted to get a picture of Big Foot! They came from all over just to lay eyes on him.

Seriously, what's the big deal about being big? Frank really wanted to know.

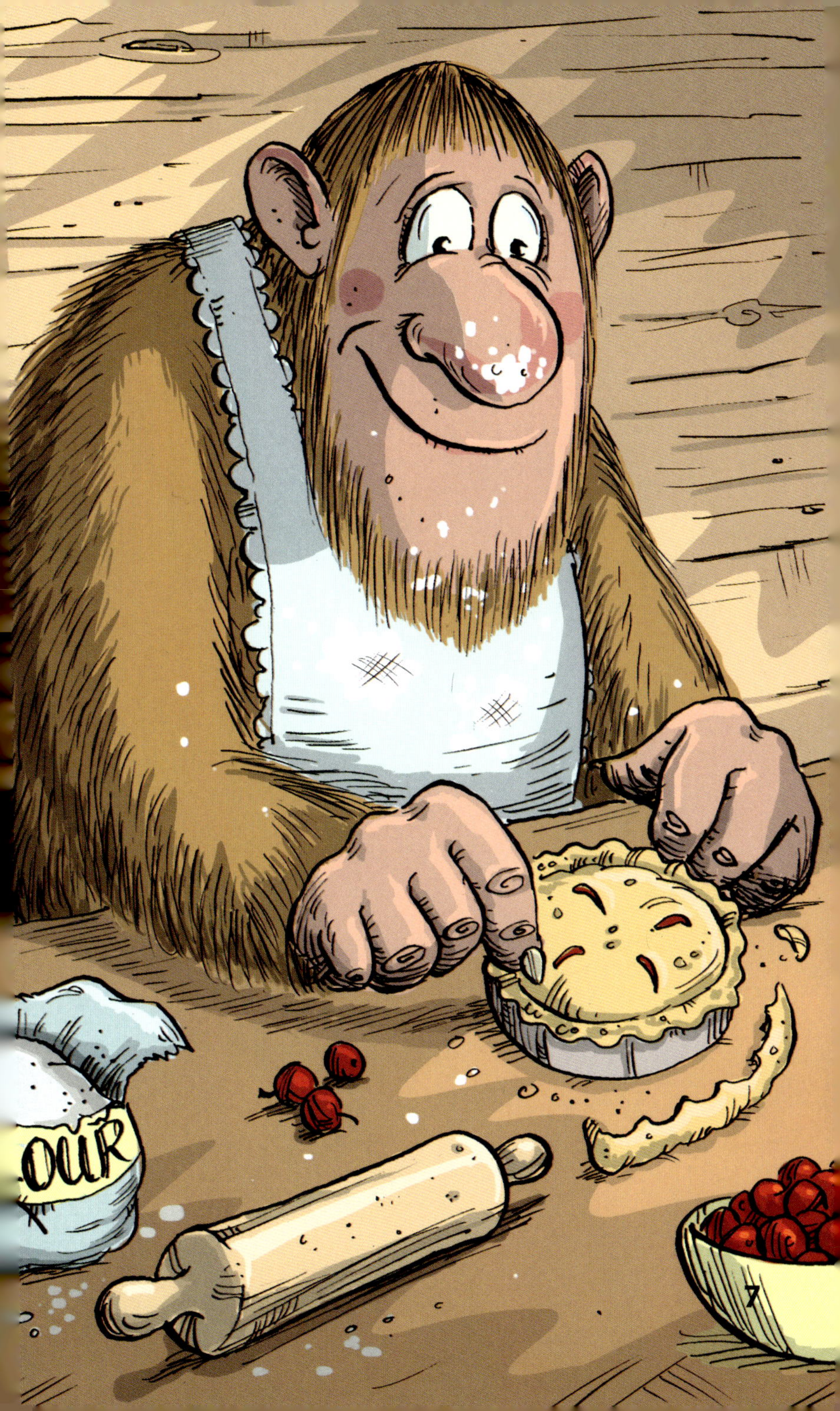
OUR

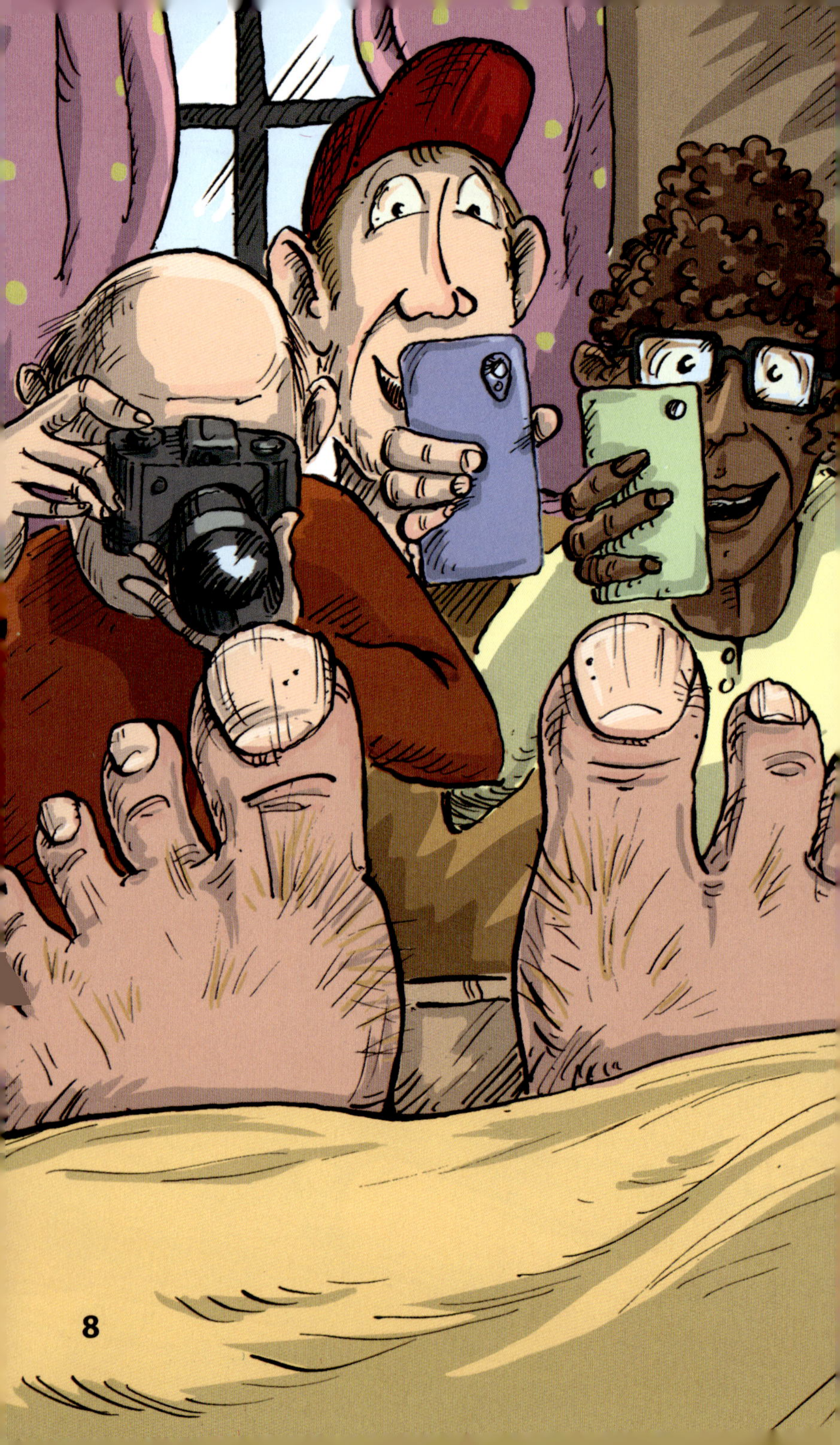

Oh, he knew he was being cranky. He was overworked and overtired. It was hard to catch a break with everyone clamoring to spot him. He once woke up from a nap with three camera-toting tourists surrounding his bed, trying to take photos of him asleep—drool and all.

Fortunately, he woke up just in time to bash their cameras and send them on their way. But really, bashing cameras wasn't much fun, and it didn't make him feel any better. And now that everyone had smartphones, there was no getting away from the paparazzi.

He needed to get away from it all and just be Frank for a while and not Big Foot.

“That’s it!” Frank called out, startling a tourist group from Miami who were trying to catch a glimpse of him through the trees. “I know what I need. A vacation!”

And that’s how Frank’s adventure began.

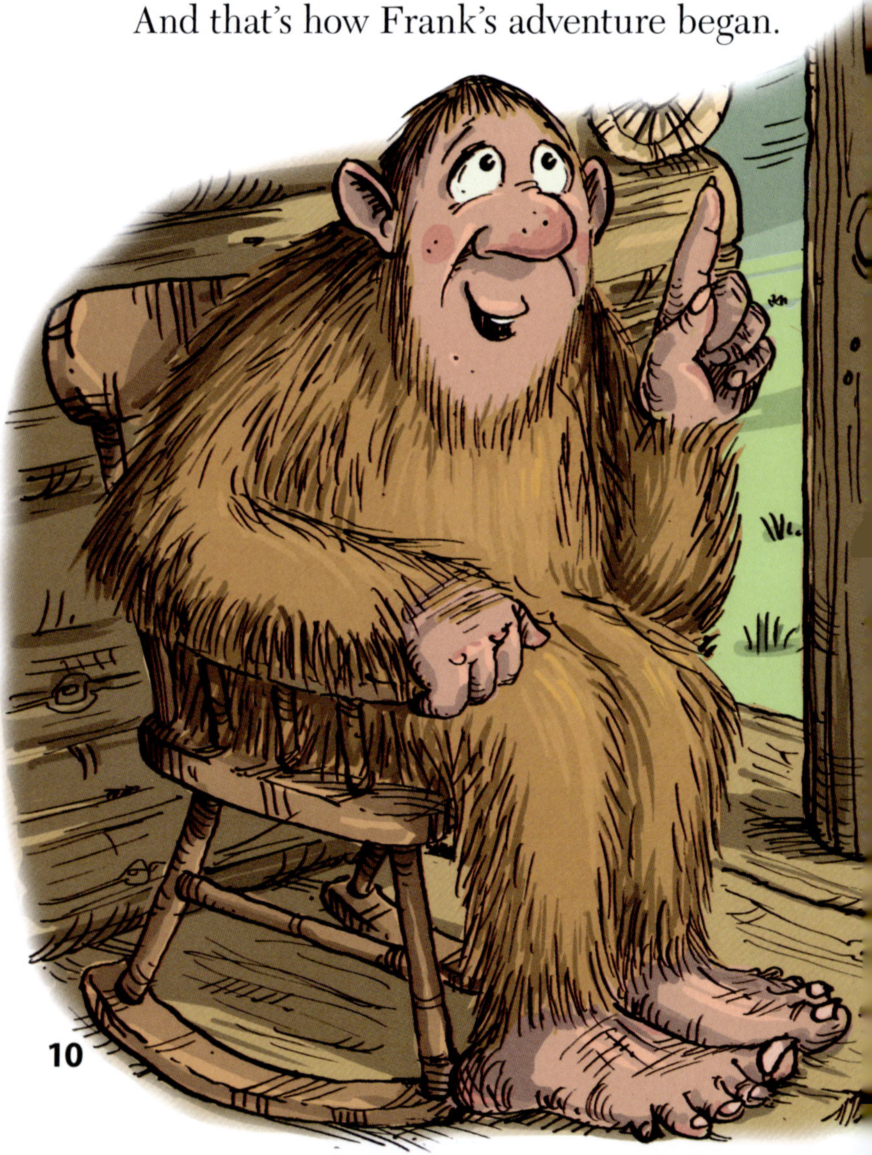

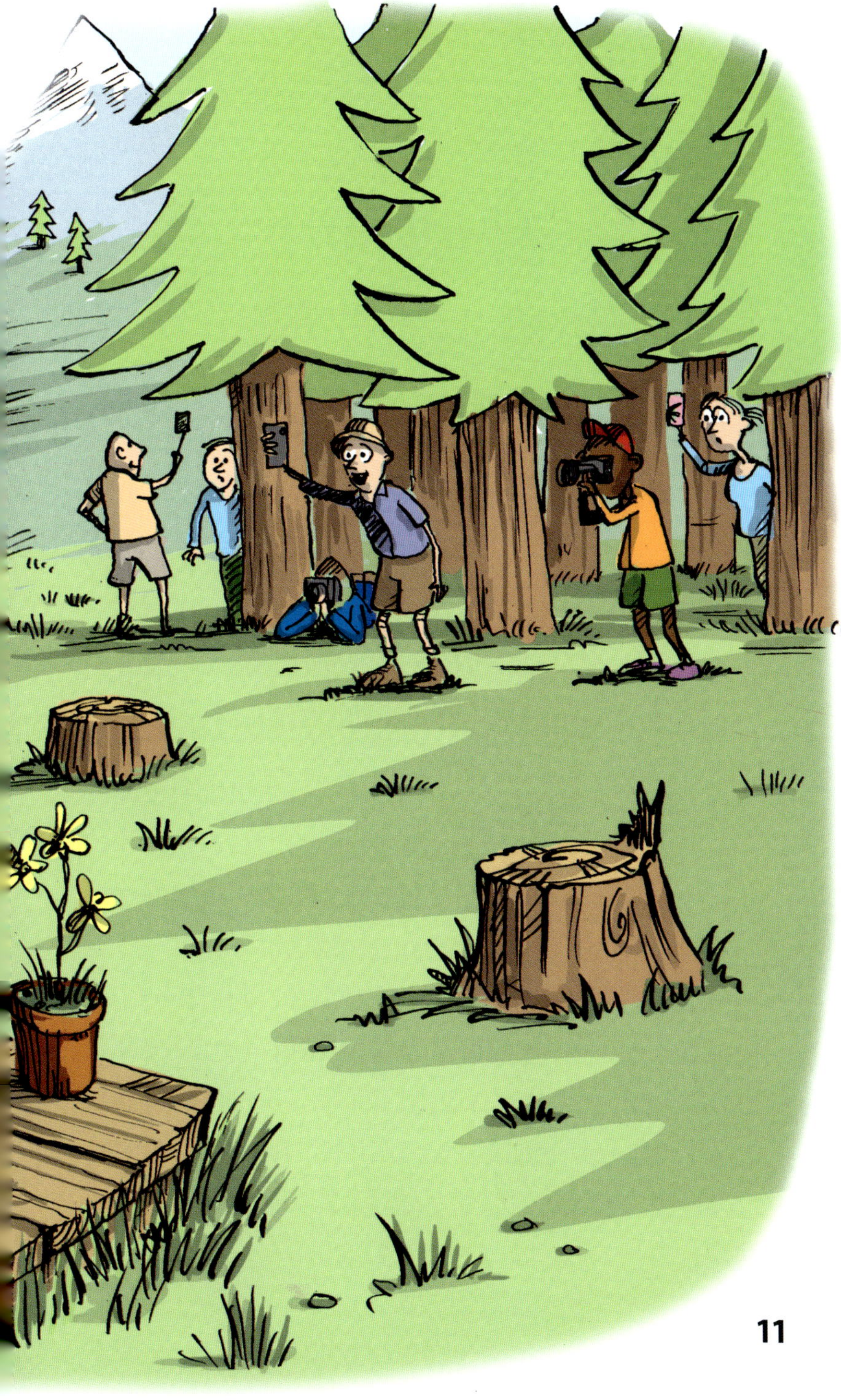

Chapter Two

See the World

Frank sat down that night to make a travel plan. He wanted to see all the big places in the world. He hoped he would fit in and no one would notice him.

First, he went online to book his flights. He learned that the airplane offered seats with extra legroom! He booked his tickets right away. Next, he packed his bag, including a lot of black clothes. He had heard wearing black might help him look slim. Maybe he would seem a lot smaller and not be noticed as much. It was worth a shot, anyway.

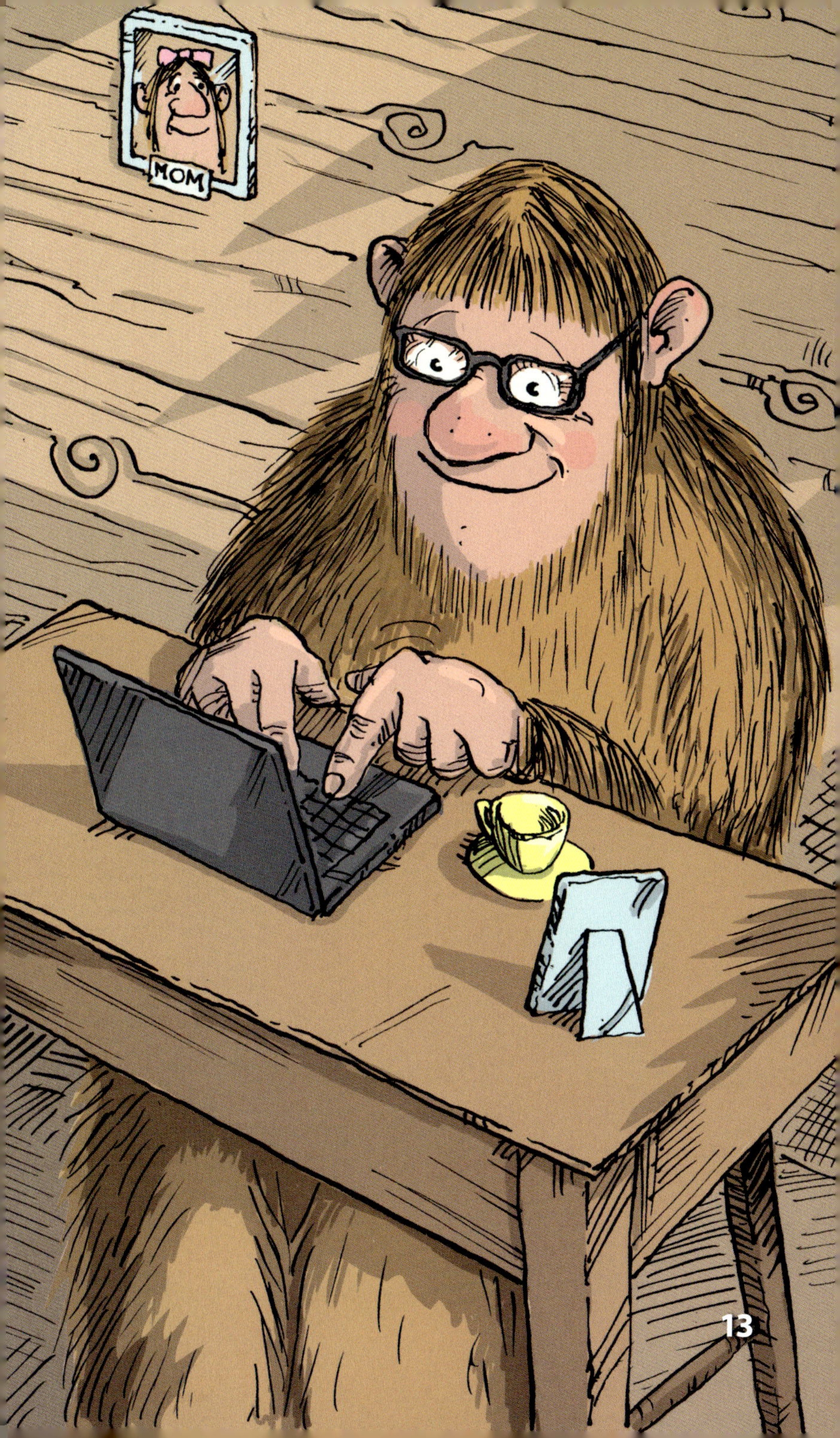
MOM

At the San Francisco airport—the closest one to Frank's house—things did not begin as well as he had hoped. Everyone was super excited to see Big Foot in person. All the blinking flashes had Frank seeing spots as he made his way to his boarding gate.

And once on the plane, those extra legroom seats weren't all they were cracked up to be! Good thing Frank's row was empty so he could stretch out a bit.

Frank was a heavy sleeper, so he slept through most of the 10-hour flight. When the plane landed, he was well-rested and ready to enjoy Paris, France! He took a taxi straight to the Eiffel Tower. It was big and magnificent, and Frank was delighted to see it. Of course, all the tourists started snapping his photo right away. Frank had to skip out of sight to avoid being grabbed by his fans. *"Le Big Foot!"* they cried, chasing him all the way to the Champs-Elysées. He ducked around the Arc de Triomphe and lost them.

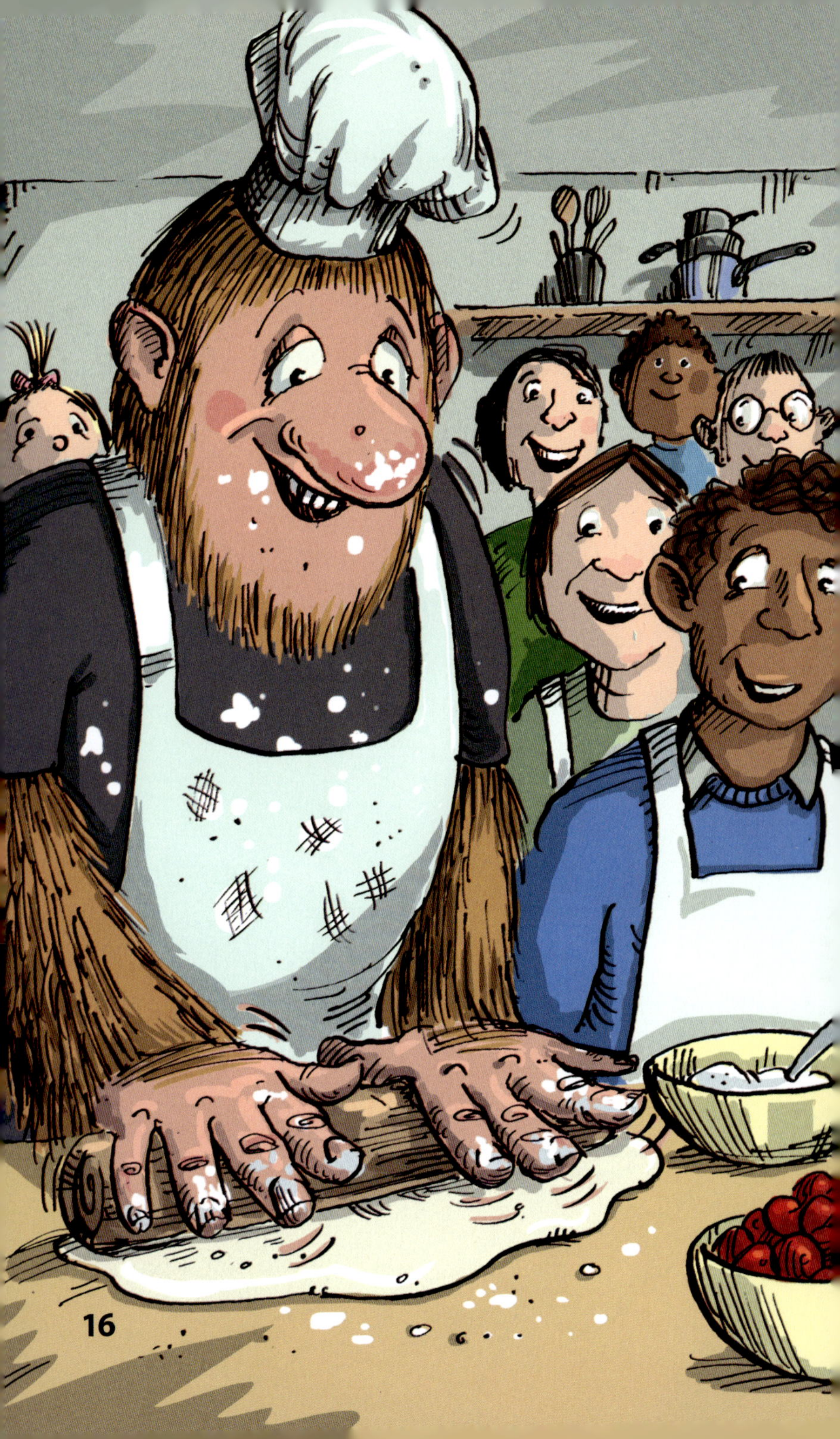

"Whew!" Frank said, sitting down on his suitcase and wiping his brow. "What will I do now?"

Just then, a paper skittered past Frank's feet, caught in a sudden breeze. He picked it up and read it. He had learned the language in the French-Canadian wilderness with his old friend Sasquatch. The paper said that there was a pie-baking class that very day right down the street. Frank had heard the French were well-known for their cooking. He decided to give the class a try.

Pie baking was exactly what Frank needed to lift his spirits. His crust-making technique was a hit with the class. And for the first time, Frank made friends with not-so-big folks. Now, that was something new! He was ready for the next phase of his trip. Onward to the Amazon rainforest!

Chapter Three

Get the Picture

The flight to Peru was just as expected, and the people at the airport were just as starstruck. *"Pie Grande!"* they called. But Frank didn't seem to mind quite so much. He texted his new pie-making friends about it, and they all had a laugh. It was nice to laugh with friends.

Once Frank arrived at the rainforest, he was having a great time. The unique animals and the beautiful plants and flowers were worth the trip.

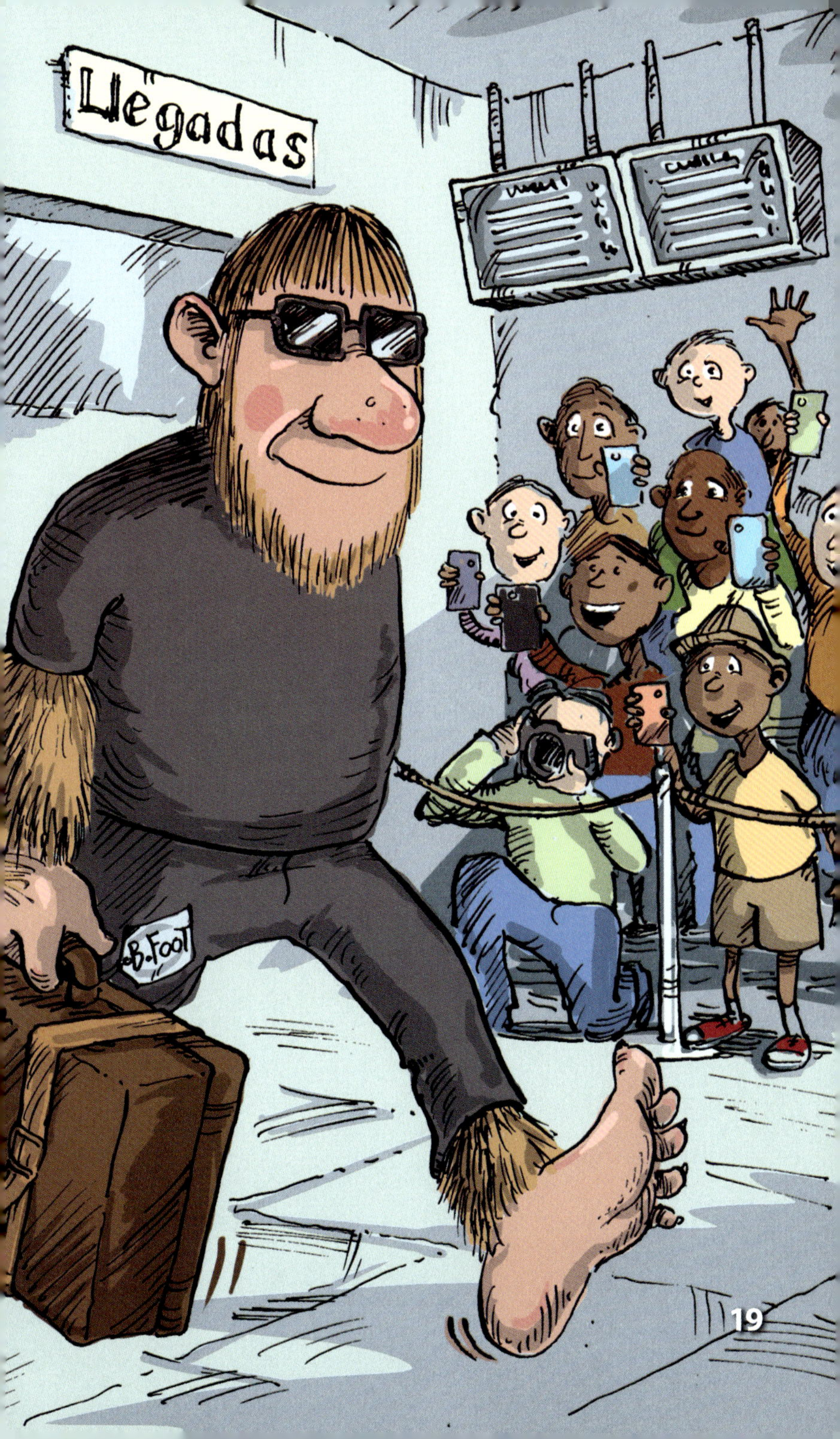
Llegadas
B.FOOT

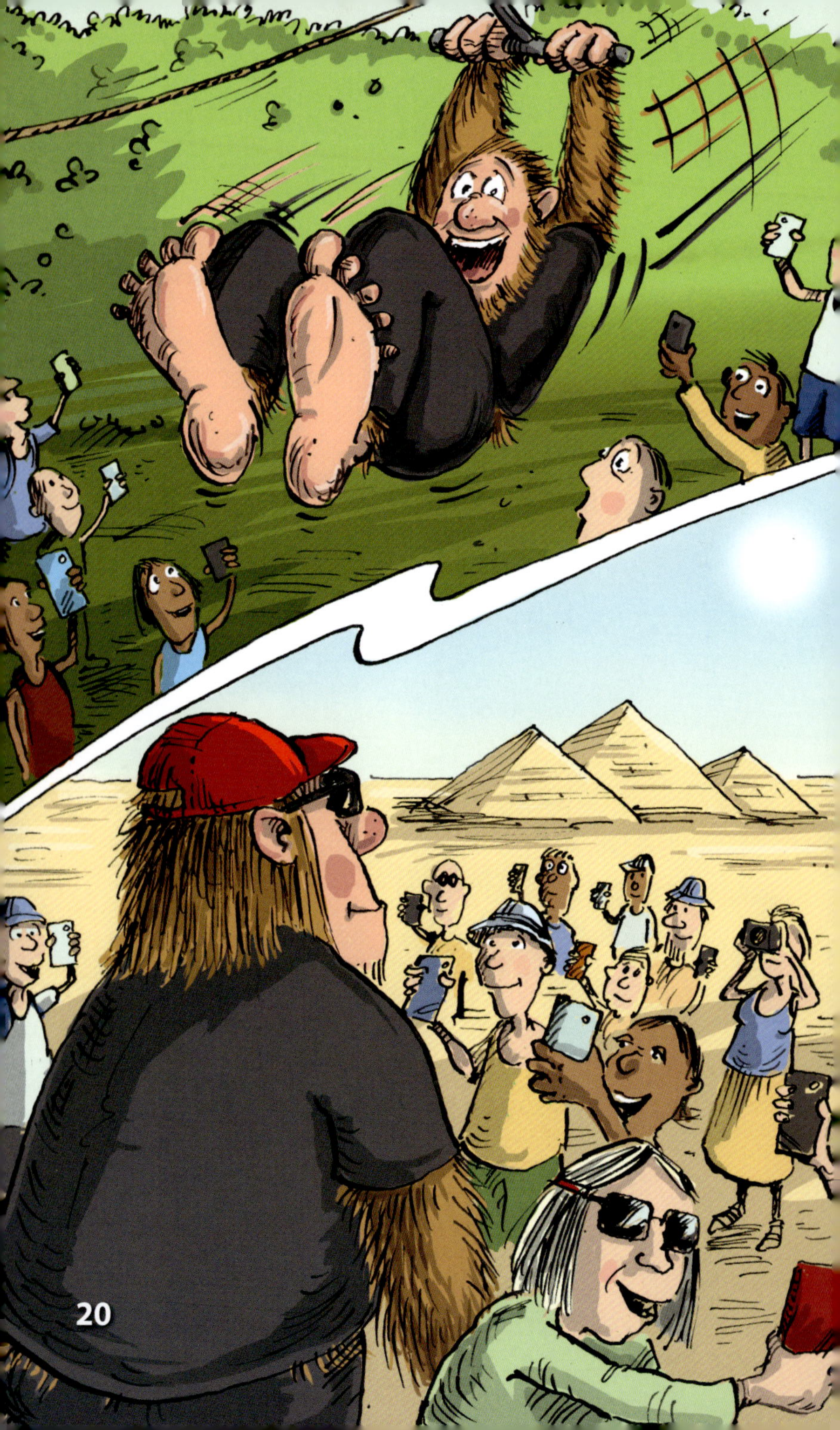

Frank was glad to be so big in such a big place. It let him see farther up into the trees than most people could. And riding the zip line was about as much fun as his big feet could handle!

From Peru, Frank headed to Egypt to see the great pyramids. Some people took his picture as he went, but he didn't pay much attention to them. The world was an interesting place, Frank found, and he was happy to see it. He got a bird's-eye view. He even took some photos for other tourists of things they couldn't see!

Little by little, he started to chat with the other travelers. They learned that "Big Foot" really *was* a sparkling conversationalist. And Frank learned that people were excited to just see him. He even posed for a photo or two with them.

Frank left Egypt and headed for Japan. He had always wanted to see Mount Fuji. It didn't disappoint! Frank learned that he also loved sushi. He ate a lot of sushi in Japan. The sushi chefs were amazing. Frank even asked if *he* could take a picture with *them*.

There were a lot of great sights in Japan, and Frank tried to see them all. He was having the time of his life!

In fact, he was having so much fun that he playfully photobombed some other people's photos. Everyone laughed. More new friends!

One of these new friends gave Frank a gift. The people of Japan invented some pretty great gadgets. Frank's friend thought one gadget might come in handy with Frank's new interest in photos. It was a selfie stick. Frank quickly got the hang of it.

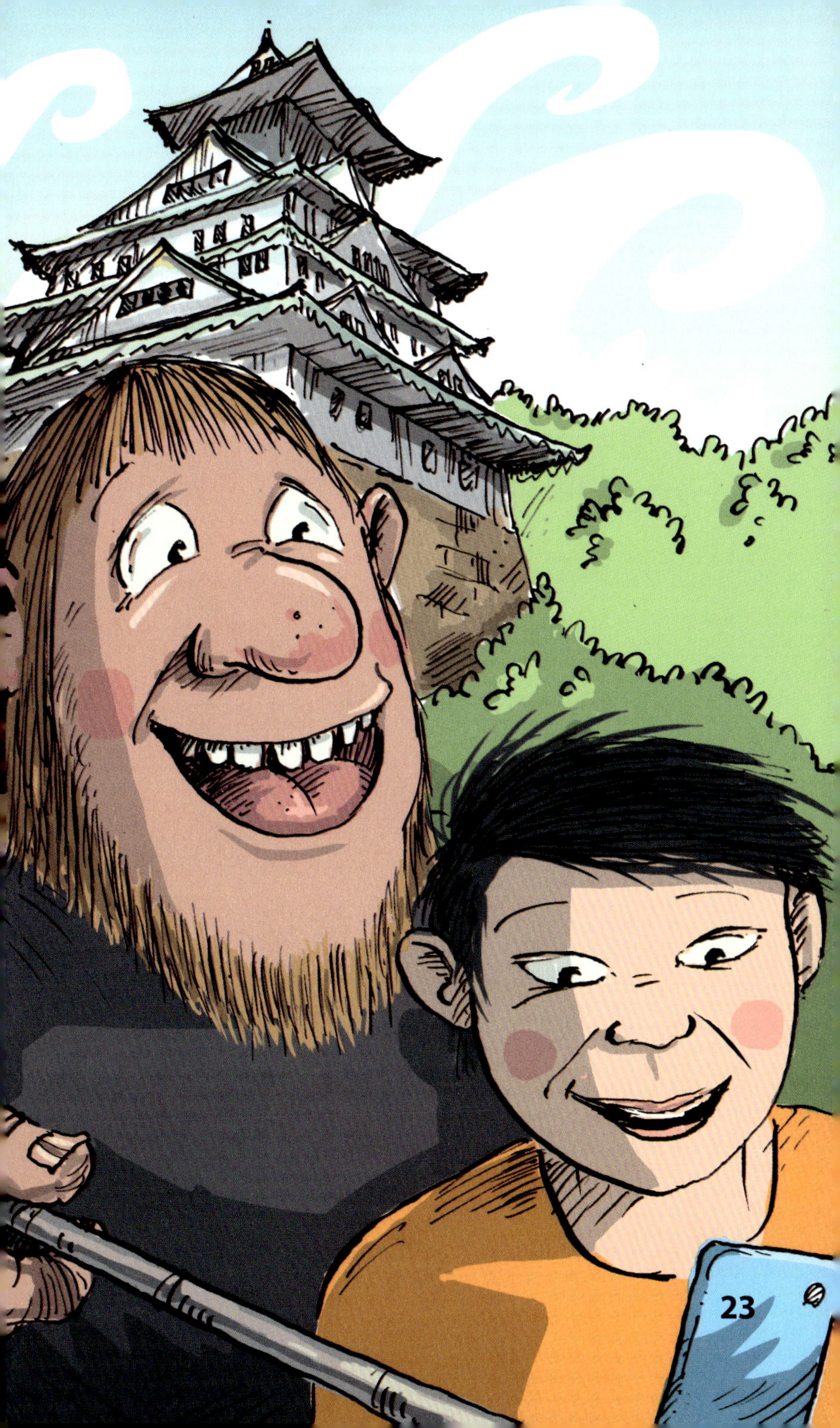

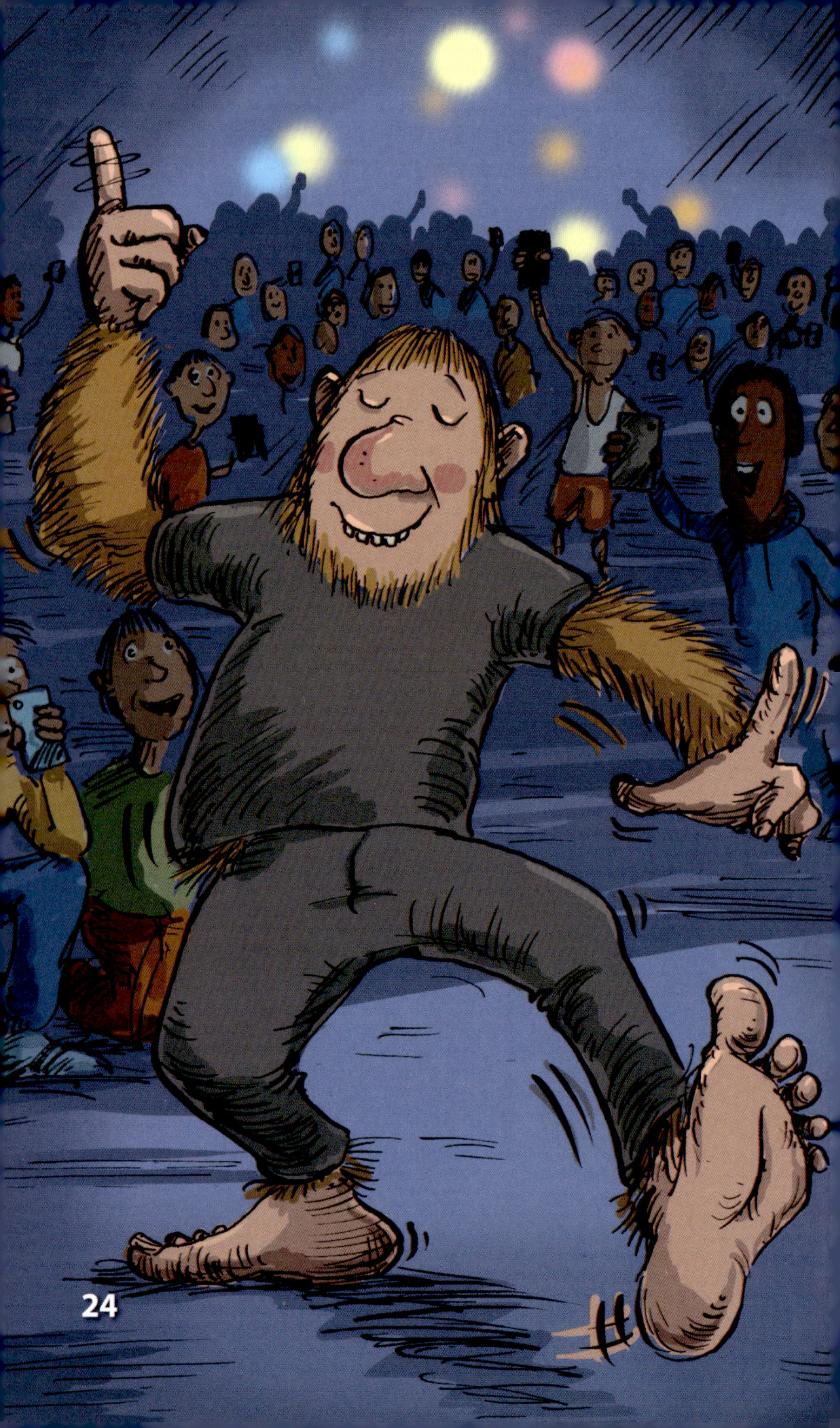

The selfie stick was useful at Frank's next stop. He wanted to see the giant Hollywood Sign for himself. Now, he could easily snap a photo of himself and put it in his memory book. And the people of Hollywood were no trouble at all. There were celebrities everywhere, so Frank was just one of the crowd. And they all loved to take selfies, just like Frank did. *More friends!* Cameras were all around, and Frank didn't mind in the least. When he went to a Hollywood dance club that night, he was happy for all his new friends to take photos of him and his fancy dance moves.

Frank had traveled around the world and was so glad he did. He made new friends everywhere. He saved his memories through photos. Frank was heading home a changed man, refreshed and happy.

And that gave Frank a great new idea.

Chapter Four

Frank Lands on His Feet

Frank touched down at the airport with a plan, and he got right to work.

First, he gave Sasquatch a call. He explained his idea and asked Sas to be his partner. Sas loved the plan! He said he would pack up and move there right away.

Next, Frank found a little shop for rent near a giant grove of redwood trees. Perfect. With the right equipment, it would be just the thing he needed. He signed a lease then and there.

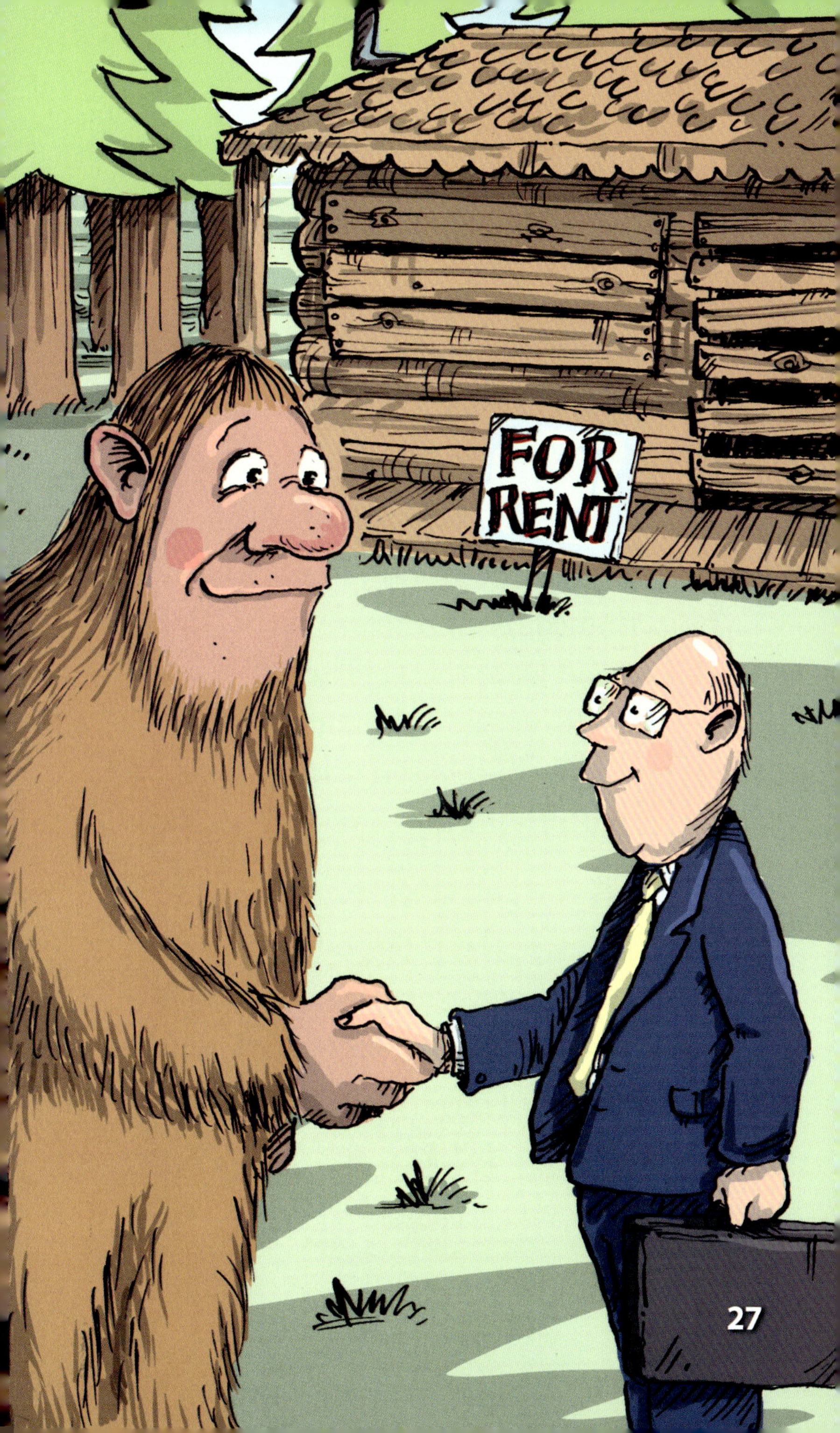
FOR RENT

When Sas arrived, they worked together to get ready. They put in the equipment, got the ingredients, and made a sign: "Big Foot's Picture-Perfect Pies." Yes, Big Foot. Frank no longer disliked the nickname after his trip. He realized it fit him perfectly!

The day they opened, people came from all over the world. Frank's friends from France, Peru, Egypt, Japan, and Hollywood were there. They all wanted a taste of Frank's world-famous pies. And for every pie purchased, the customer got a photo with Frank and Sas!

Frank turned on the twinkle lights he'd strung in the redwoods. They lit up a dance floor, where Frank and his customers danced the night away under the lights. Frank and his big feet couldn't have been happier.

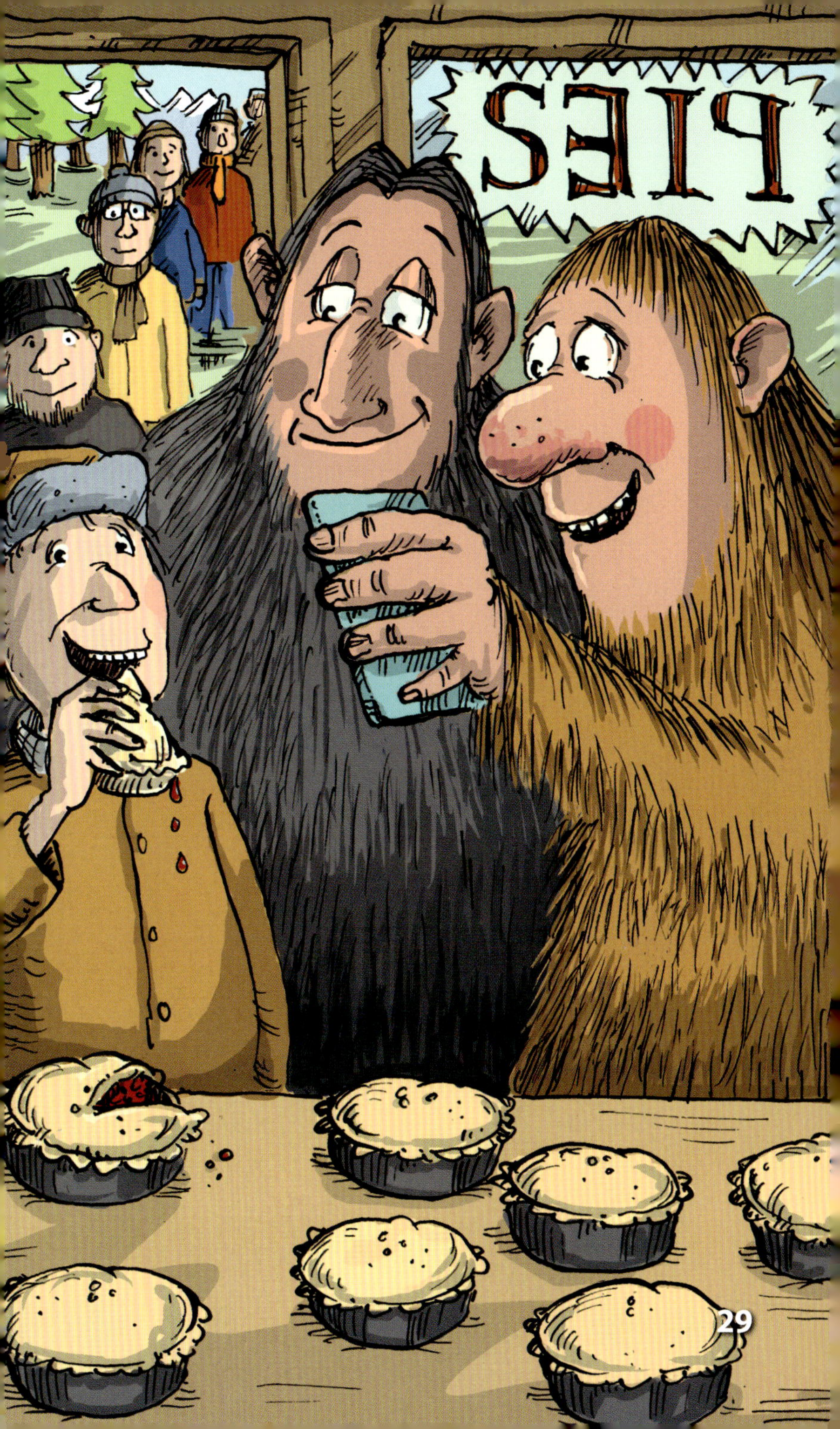
PIES

Was Frank's life picture perfect?

Well, yes, Frank thought as he danced. *It is perfect. And it's good to be me, big feet and all!*

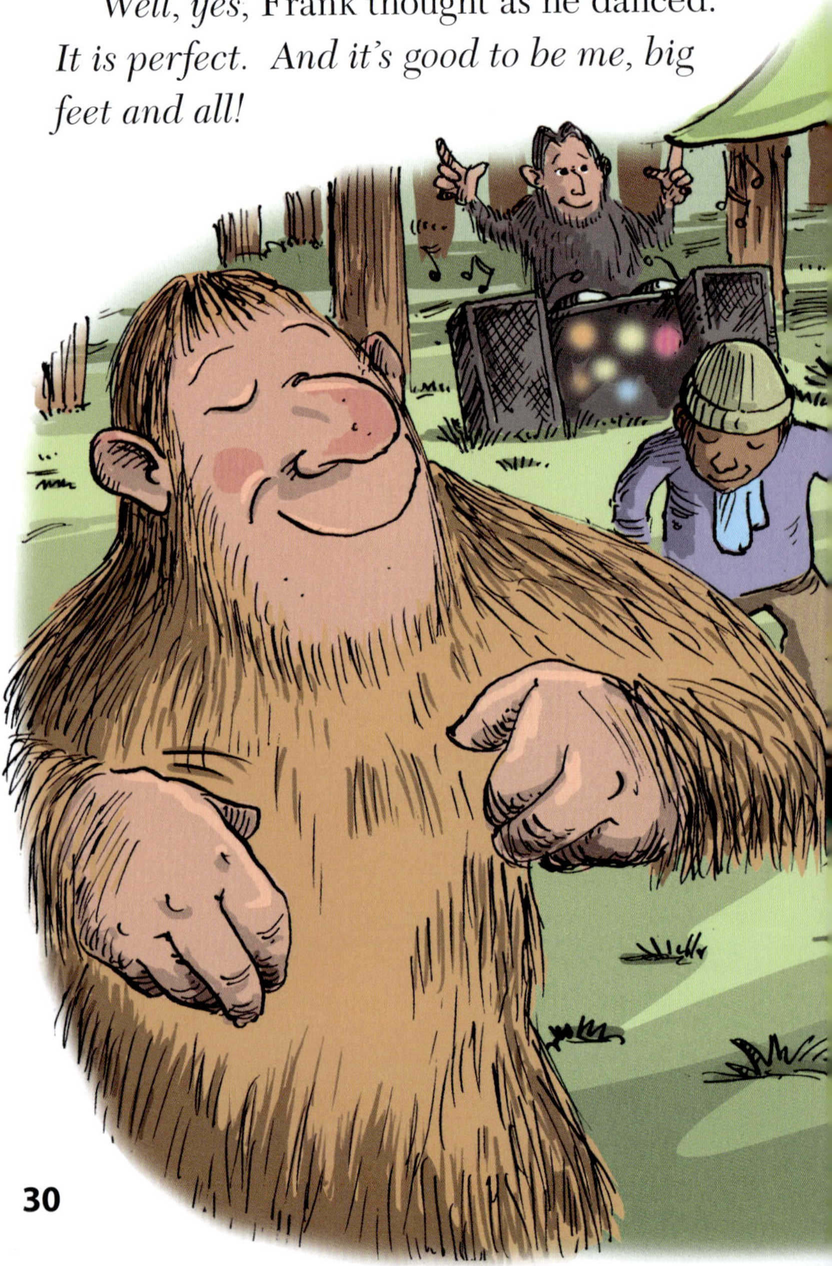

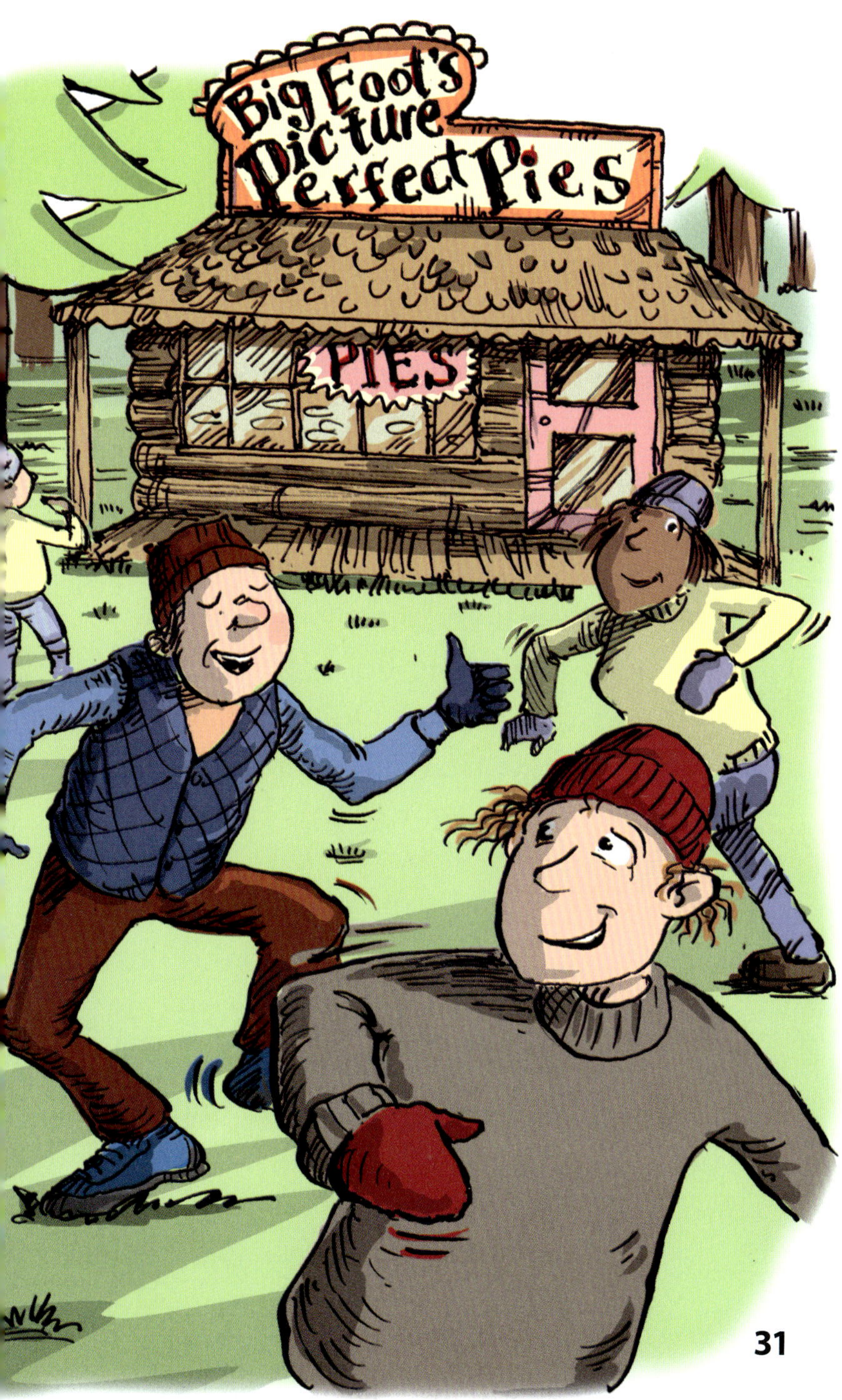
Big Foot's Picture Perfect Pies
PIES

About Us

The Author
Dona Herweck Rice is a California-based writer who has written hundreds of books for children of all ages on just about every topic under the sun. This isn't even her first book on Big Foot. Even so, she is delighted to have written it, especially as one of her nephews is a devoted Big Foot hunter. He's just certain there are Big Foots (*Big Feet?*) out there somewhere. Dona is glad to tell her nephew that she spotted one—right inside the pages of this book!

The Illustrator
Sholto Walker grew up in England, just steps from the sea. When he wasn't on the beach, he was in his room taking things apart or drawing. He is happiest when he can take an idea and turn it into a picture.